GODLY DECLARATIONS:

SPEAK LIFE INTO YOUR SITUATIONS

Tola Dehinde

GODLY DECLARATIONS:

SPEAK LIFE INTO YOUR SITUATIONS

COPYRIGHT

APPRECIATION & DEDICATION

I thank God for the Word of life that flows throughout the Bible.

I thank the Holy Spirit for opening my eyes to see the importance of speaking life into my circumstances.

I appreciate the Holy Spirit who has helped me to write this book.

I would also like to thank everyone who has encouraged me to write.

This book is dedicated to you reading it.

Table of Contents

INTRODUCTION

Sometimes, when I feel low or discouraged, I have periods when I just cannot pray. It is at those times, that I read the Bible. As I searched the Scriptures, I found out that I can confess words of life, by that I mean speak Scriptures and know that by doing so, I am speaking things into being. In Jonh 1:1 _In the beginning was the Word_, and the Word was with God, and the Word was God. ² He was with God in the beginning. ³ Through him all things were made; without him nothing was made that has been made. ⁴ In him was life, and that life was the light of all mankind. ¹⁴ _The Word became flesh_ and made his dwelling among us. We have seen his glory, the glory of the one and only Son, who came from the Father, full of grace and truth.

As a believer, God says He has given us authority and power in Luke 10: ¹⁹ Behold, I give you the authority to trample on serpents and scorpions, and over all the power of the enemy, and nothing shall by any means hurt you. This verse empowers us to exercise our authority over every aspect of our lives that we are not happy about.

Underline for emphasis by author

The power that Jesus has given us, is a spiritual and verbal one, to decree, to command, to proclaim, to build up, to tear down and shift the authority back to us. This authority if we exercise it, will not allow the enemy to have victory over us.

In Romans 10:*10 For with the heart one believes unto righteousness, and with the mouth confession is made unto salvation.* When we confess with our mouths, we are saved. Further on, in verse *17 So then faith comes by hearing, and hearing by the word of God.* Irrespective of how you hear the Word of Christ, even if it is by you confessing it, you are building up your faith.

The Bible is filled with passages about us speaking 'life words' to ourselves. As Christians, that is what God wants us to do. We are used to saying AMEN to men and women of God blessing us are we not? Let us also bless ourselves during our quiet times.

Ezekiel chapter 37 is one of those chapters, where God shows us the power of the spoken word. The potency of prophesy is so strong that we can speak to any dead situation we are in or our loved ones are in. In this chapter we see that God can give life through His Word and His breath, which is the Spirit of God.

Ezekiel 37: 1 The hand of the Lord came upon me and brought me out in the Spirit of the Lord, and set me down in the midst of the valley; and it was full of bones. 2 Then He caused me to pass by them all around, and behold, there were very many in the open valley; and indeed they were very dry. 3 And He said to me, "Son of man, can these bones live?" So I answered, "O Lord God, You know." 4 Again He said to me, "<u>Prophesy to these bones,</u> and say to them, 'O dry bones, hear the word of the Lord! 5 Thus says the Lord God to these bones: "Surely I will cause breath to enter into you, and you shall live.   6 I will put sinews on you and bring flesh upon you, cover you with skin and put breath in you; and you shall live. Then you shall know that I am the Lord." ' "7 So I prophesied as I was commanded; <u>and as I prophesied, there was a noise</u>, and suddenly a rattling; and the bones came together, bone to bone. 8 Indeed, as I looked, the sinews and the flesh came upon them, and the skin covered them over; but there was no breath in them.   9 Also He said to me, "<u>Prophesy to the breath, prophesy, son of man</u>, and say to the breath, 'Thus says the Lord God: "Come from the four winds, O breath, and breathe on these slain, that they may live." 10 <u>So I prophesied</u> as He commanded me, and breath came into them, and they lived, and stood upon their feet, an exceedingly great army.

God wants us to speak life to our dry bones. God wants us to form the habit of regularly blessing ourselves by speaking words of life. Proverbs 18:21 tells us that *Death and life are in the power of the tongue, And those who love it will eat its fruit.* God created the heavens and the earth by the power of the spoken word. Gen 1:3 *Then God said, "Let there be light"; and there was light.*

The power of the tongue is so important in the life of a believer, in terms of what we say about ourselves, to ourselves, to our children and to situations around us. Let's develop the habit of speaking life to our circumstances no matter how desperate the matter might seem.

In John chapter 11, we read the story of Lazarus, the brother of Mary and Martha. He was sick and died. When Jesus heard about his death, Jesus was out of town and by this time, Lazarus was buried. Jesus finally made his way back to town and to the siblings' home. A crowd was gathering as Jesus went to the tomb where Lazarus was buried. When Jesus got there, in verse 39, Jesus said *"Take away the stone."* Jesus Himself spoke words in season, Rhema words and words of life! Be inspired.

In Isaiah 55: 11 *So shall My word be that goes forth from My mouth; It shall not return to Me void, But it shall accomplish what I please, And it shall prosper in the thing for which I sent it.* The Lord is telling us that anything He says will not return to Him void. We are followers of our Lord Jesus Christ, if it works for Him, it will work for us. If God says words will not return void to Him, then it will be the same for us as we speak words of life too, according to His will and purpose.

In Philippians 4:6 we are told *Be anxious for nothing, but in everything by prayer and supplication, with thanksgiving, let your requests be made known to God.* Even as we confess the word of life, our request, confessions, declarations, blessings have to be made known to God.

As you confess these Scriptures, do not rush over them; take your time and let them sink into your spirit soul and into your body. 2 Corinthians 4:*13 It is written: I believed; therefore I have spoken. Since we have that same spirit of faith, we also believe and therefore speak.*

Remember you are speaking life!

WORSHIP HIS MAJESTY

Revelation 4:10-11 *The four and twenty elders fall down before him that sat on the throne, and worship him that lives for every and ever, and cast their crowns before the throne, saying. You are worth, our Lord and God, to receive glory and honour and power, for you created all things, and by your will they were created and have their being."*

Our God is worthy to be praised at all times.

Declarations:

Lord you are the Son of the Highest. You are a great King over all the earth. Lord you are the Light of the world. You are the man of war. The Lord God Omnipotent reigns. Rose of Sharon and the Lily of the Valley. I AM that I AM.

You are the God who kills and makes alive. A Sceptre of Righteousness. God of Peace. The Great Shepherd of the sheep. You are the Way, the Truth and Life. The Firstborn from the dead. Lord God Almighty, which was, and is and is to come. Lord of heaven and earth. The Stem of Jesse.

Alleluia! Salvation and glory and honour and power belong to the Lord our God.

The God of gods and the Lord of kings and a revealer of secrets. The faithful God, the Covenant keeping God. The Lion of Judah and the Root of David. Heaven is your throne and the earth your footstool.

The Author and Finisher of our faith. You are Alpha and Omega, the Beginning and the Ending. The First and the Last. The Root and offspring of David, the Bright and Morning Star.

For the Lord is great and greatly to be praised. Honour and majesty are before your Lord. Strength and beauty are in your sanctuary. I worship you in the beauty of holiness.

I will extol you my God, my King, and I will bless your name forever. Great is the Lord and greatly to be praised; the Lord's greatness is unsearchable. Lord you are gracious and full of compassion.

References:

Acts 7:49

Colossians 1:18

Daniel 2:47

Deuteronomy 7:9; 32:39

Exodus 3:14; 15:3

Hebrews 1:8; 12: 2; 13:20

Isaiah 11:1

John 9:5; 14:6

Luke 1:32

Matthew 11:25

Psalm 47:2; 96:4&6; 145:1, 3 & 8;

Revelation 1:6 & 11; 5:5; 11:17; 19:1&6; 22:16

Song 2:11

BIBLICAL BLESSINGS

The Bible is full of the Word of God blessing us all. I am an avid reader of the Bible, because I am always on the lookout for a scripture that touches my heart that I can use when it is time for my Bible study or when I am praying. When Satan tempted Jesus, our Lord Jesus used Scriptures to answer Satan back.

In Galatians 3: *13 Christ has redeemed us from the curse of the law, having become a curse for us (for it is written, Cursed is everyone who hangs on a tree"), 14 that the blessing of Abraham might come upon the Gentiles in Christ Jesus, that we might receive the promise of the Spirit through faith.* This verse tells us that Abraham's blessings of justification by faith might come to us Gentiles. The Word of God is living and powerful.

Declarations:

The Lord bless me, the Lord make me fruitful and multiply me. May I find grace in the eyes the Lord, like Noah. I will reap bountifully because I have sown bountifully. Let my light break forth like the morning, let my healing spring forth speedily, let my righteousness go before me and the glory of God be my rear guard. My hope will not be cut off.

Lord make me alive and bring me up; Lord make me rich and lift me up; Lord raise me up out of the dust and set me among princes and make me inherit the throne of glory. Though my beginning was small, yet my latter days shall increase abundantly. The Lord my God will make me abound in all the work of my hands, in the fruit of my body, in the increase of my bank account and in the produce of my land for good.

I am the head and not the tail, above and not beneath. I am more than a conqueror through Christ who loves me. My body is the temple of the Holy Spirit. I am blessed because I trust in the Lord. My life will be brighter than the noonday.

Father heal me and reveal to me the abundance of peace and truth. I will be satisfied with God's goodness. Lord do better for me than my beginnings. Because I wait on the Lord, I will renew my strength, I shall mount up with wings like eagles, I shall run and not be weary, I shall walk and not faint. Lord hasten your Word to perform it. The Lord will satisfy me with long life.

There is therefore now no condemnation to me because I am in Christ Jesus and I walk not after the flesh but after the Spirit. In everything I am enriched by Him, in all utterance and in all knowledge. Blessed be the God and Father of my Lord Jesus Christ, who has blessed me with all spiritual blessings in heavenly places in Christ.

After I have suffered a while, may the God of all grace, who called me to His eternal glory by Christ Jesus, perfect, establish, strengthen and settle me in Jesus name.

Prayers:

Father Lord, let your Words bring life into my situation (name the situation) in Jesus name.

Lord I want to know you more as I declare your Words of life.

I have made this declaration by faith and by faith I will receive an answer in Jesus name.

References:

Deuteronomy 30:9; 28:13

Ephesians 1:3

Ezekiel 6:11

Genesis 1:28; 6:8

Jeremiah 33:6; 31:13; 31:14; 1:12

Proverb 16:20b; 23:18

Psalm 91:16

Hebrews 4:12

Isaiah 58:8; 40:31

Job 8:7; 11:17

Roman 8:1& 37

2 Corinthians 9:6

1Corinthians 1:5 6:19

1 Peter 5:10

1 Samuel 2:6-8

CONFESSIONS FOR THE NEW MONTH

This is one of my monthly confession. Job 38:12 *"Have you commanded the morning since your days began, and caused the dawn to know its place.* This verse tells us what we need to do first thing in the morning, command our day.

Declarations:

This month, My God shall supply all of my needs according to His riches in glory by Christ Jesus. I (insert your name) will expand to the right and to the left. The Lord satisfies my mouth with good things, my youth is renewed like the eagles. I (insert your name) will take root downwards and bear fruit upwards.

I will build houses and inhabit, I will plant and eat the fruit of them; I will not build and another inhabit, I will not plant for another to eat, for as the days of a tree are, I will long enjoy, as God's elect the work of my hands. I will not labour in vain this new month.

The Lord will bring me out into a broad place this month; He delivered me because He delights in me. My soul shall be satisfied as with marrow and fatness, and my mouth shall praise you with joyful lips.

This month, the Lord will make me lay down in green pastures. The Lord gives me the dew of Heaven and of the fatness of the earth, and plenty to eat and drink. The Lord God will help me; therefore I will not be disgraced; therefore I have set my face like a flint, and I know that I will not be ashamed.

This month, the Lord make me fruitful and multiply me. May I find grace in the eyes of the Lord like Moses did in Jesus name. Father you are faithful and you will establish me and keep me from evil.

This month, I (insert your name) will begin to prosper, I will continue prospering till I become very prosperous like Isaac. I will reap bountifully because I have sown bountifully. This month, I will arise and shine for my light has come and the glory of the Lord is risen upon me.

My hope for this month, will not be cut off. Lord make me alive and bring me up; Lord make me rich and lift me up; Lord raise me up out of the dust and set me among the princes and make me inherit the throne of glory.

The Lord my God will make me abound in all the work of my hands, in the fruit of my body and in the produce of my land for good. This month Lord restore to me the years that the locust has eaten, the cankerworm, and the caterpillar, and the palmerworm. So shall it be in Jesus matchless name.

This month, I will bring forth new fruit. Let the windows of heaven be opened unto me this month and I declare that I will lack nothing. I will delight myself in the Lord and He will give me the desires of my heart.

Prayer:

I lift up this month up before you Lord and I ask for your divine protection in Jesus name.

Lord help me to get closer to you this month.

Lord enlarge the place of my dwelling in Jesus name.

Reference:

Deuteronomy 30:9

Exodus 3:13

Ezekiel 30:22 & 36:11b & 47:12

Genesis 1:28; 6:8; 26:13; 27:28

Isaiah 37:31; 50:7; 54: 2 & 3; 58:8; 60:1; 65:21 – 23

Joel 2:23

Philippians 4:19

Psalms 18:19; 23:2; 37:4; 63:5.103:5;

Proverb 23:18

2 Corinthians 9:6

1 Kings 4:27

1 Samuel 2:6-8

 2 Thessalonians 3:3

CONFESSIONS FOR YOUR CHILDREN

Parents always wish their children well and want the best for them. Praying God's Words over them is a good way to do this. Cultivate the habit of speaking life over your child or children and praying to God for them.

Children are going through so much. The world we live in is not helping, there is a lot of temptation over the internet. Children are experiencing mental health issues at an alarming rate. There are temptations all around them. Thank goodness we can lift our voices up to God as parents and care-givers.

Parents worry over their child/ren all the time. The times that we live in is calamitous. What better way to take the burden off you as a parent, by speaking faith in God's Word into your child/ren life.

There is supernatural authority in declaring God's Words over your children.

Declarations:

Father God, I thank you for your goodness to me and to my children. I thank you Lord for the children that you have graciously blessed me with.

I thank you Lord that your mercy is from everlasting to everlasting and that your righteousness are upon my children because I fear you.

I thank you Lord that you will give my children increase more and more in Jesus name. Thank you Lord that my children are a heritage from you. I thank you Lord that as I walk in integrity, my children are blessed after me. I thank you Lord for the children that you have given me and we are for signs and wonders.

Thank you Lord for your promise to save my children. Thank you Lord for saving my children. Thank you Lord, that you will help me to train my child/ren so, that he/she/them will not depart from you.

I thank you Lord that you will teach all my children and my children shall be at peace in Jesus name. I will not bring children for trouble, for I am a descendants of the blessed of the Lord, and my offspring with them.

Lord let my children keep the way of the Lord, to do justice and judgement. Lord visit my children and let them be fruitful and let them increase abundantly and let them multiply and wax exceedingly mighty.

Father God look upon my children and have respect unto them. Lord let my children learn to fear the Lord my God. Lord let my children be blessed with children. Father God, save my children. Lord let you righteousness be upon my children's children.

The Lord Himself watches over my children. The Lord stands beside her/him/them as a protective shade. The sun will not harm them by day not the moon by night. My children will delight to do your will O my God and your law will be within their hearts.

Let my children be like olive plants roundabout my table. By your mercy Lord do not let me know the loss of my children. Father God give my children knowledge and skill in all learning and wisdom. As for me and my house, we shall serve the Lord.

Prayer:

I pray that my children will walk in truth and will be obedient children.

I pray today that my children will listen to me as I teach them the fear of the Lord.

I pray Lord that you will guide the feet of my children in Jesus name.

References:

Daniel 1:17

Deuteronomy 31:13

Exodus 1:7

Genesis 18:19; 50:28;

Isaiah 65:3

Joshua 24:15

Psalms 34:11; 33:5, 40:6; 72:4; 103:17; 107: 8; 115:4; 121:5-6; 127:3; 128:3

Proverb 20:7; 22:6

Isaiah 8:18; 47:8; 49:25; 54:13

3 John 1:4;

2nd John 1:4

1 Peter 1:14;

CONFESSIONS FOR FAMILIES

God at the beginning, created family in the Garden of Eden, Gen 2: *21 And the Lord God caused a deep sleep to fall on Adam, and he slept; and He took one of his ribs, and closed up the flesh in its place. 22 Then the rib which the Lord God had taken from man He made into a woman, and He brought her to the man.*

Family is important to God, as seen throughout the Bible. Our Lord Jesus was born into a family. In Joshua 24:15, *"But as for me and my house, we will serve the Lord."* Family is the bedrock of any society.

It is important to pray for each other and also to declare 'words of life' into the lives of our family members. Parents can speak over their children; siblings can speak over each other too and spouses can speak blessings over each other. Church family can pray for one another too.

Declarations:

Father produce in my family member (name) a clean heart; and renew your spirit within them. Let your presence abide in my family and bless all that we have. Let us learn to forgive one another. Let us put on love, which binds us all together in perfect unity as a family.

Father God I thank you that my family member (name) will not be afraid or terrified because of the battle that he/she is facing. Father I thank you that you are with my family member (name) and you will never leave nor forsake him/her/them.

Father Lord I pray that my family member (name) will walk in the authority that you have given, to trample over all the power of the enemy and according to your word nothing shall by any means hurt my family member (name).

Thank you Lord for my husband or wife who honours me and treats me with understanding as we live together in Jesus name. I know that the Lord is always with us as a family and we will not be shaken for He is right beside us.

According to your Word Lord, I come against the spirit of anxiety over my family member (name). I choose to thank you for their life/lives in Jesus name. For God has not given us a spirit of fear, but of power and love and a sound mind.

The Lord our God is with us, the Mighty Warrior who saves. He will take great delight in us; in his love He will no longer rebuke us but will rejoice over us with singing.

Let the peace of Christ rule in our hearts, since as members of one body we are called to peace and we are thankful. My children will be children in the faith. My children will be children of the light and of the day and not of the night nor of darkness. My children are heir of God through Christ.

Prayer:

Father I thank you for my family and I ask Lord that you watch over them always.

Father let us learn to forgive one another as family member/s (name them).

Father Lord, I pray your supernatural blessings over their lives in Jesus name.

References:

Colossians 3:13-14 & 15

Deuteronomy 31:6

Galatians 4:7

Luke 10:19

Psalm 16:8; 51:10

Philippians 4:6

1 Chronicles 13:14

1 Peter 3:7

1 Thessalonians 5:5

1 Timothy 1:2

2nd Timothy 1:7

Zephaniah 3:17

CONFESSIONS ON FULFILLING DESTINY

The Bible teaches that man was created with the ability to make moral choices and that he (man) is responsible for those choices. Our destiny is consequently influenced by either wanting to live in congruence with God's divine plan and following God's Words, in terms of what He wants to teach us through the Bible.

When we speak the Word of God, and decree over our Godly purpose, what we are doing in essence is terminating the effect that powers of darkness have against us as Christians. In order to experience the fulfillment of your purpose in life, you will need to pray and make decrees so that you can have dominion over the forces of darkness.

Declarations:

I make this Godly declaration and decree that I will prosper in life and do well. I am blessed. I have a sound mind and the Spirit of the Lord is upon me to run with patience the race ahead of me in life. Father God I believe you and as it was imputed unto Abraham unto righteousness, let it be so for me. I declare that I am blessed and I am highly favoured.

My steps are ordered by the Lord, And He delights in my way. Though I fall, I will not be utterly cast down; For the Lord upholds me with His hand.

For you know the thoughts that you think toward me, Lord, thoughts of peace and not of evil, to give me a future and a hope. I commit my ways to the LORD, I trust also in Him and he shall bring my plans to pass. He will bring forth my righteousness as the light and my justice as the noonday.

I am a vessel unto honour, God has a purpose for my life and it shall be made manifest in Jesus name. And I know that all things work together for my good because I love God, and I am called according to His purpose. God foreknew me, I was also predestined *to be* conformed to the image of His Son.

I will not be conformed to the pattern of this world, but I will be transformed by the renewing of my mind, that I may prove what is that good and acceptable and perfect will of God.

God's divine power has granted to me all things that pertain to life and godliness, through the knowledge of him who called me to his own glory and excellence. May God grant me according to my heart's desire and fulfill all my purpose.

Father Lord search my heart and examine my mind; to reward me according to my conduct, according to what my deeds deserve. I commit to the Lord whatever I do and He will establish my plans. The Lord will vindicate me; your love, Lord, endures forever; do not abandon the works of your hands.

I am blessed because I do not walk in the counsel of the ungodly, nor stand in the path of sinners, nor sits in the seat of the scornful; but my delight *is* in the law of the Lord, and in His law I meditate day and night. I will be like a tree planted by the rivers of water that brings forth its fruit in its season, my leaf also shall not wither; and whatever I do shall prosper.

Prayer:

Father God help me to fulfill my destiny in Jesus name.

Father I come against any power contending with my destiny.

My life will no longer be a battle ground for the enemy in Jesus name.

Reference:

Hebrews 12:1

Isaiah 65: 21-23

James 2:23

Jeremiah 17:10; 29:11

Luke 1:28

Proverbs 16: 3

Psalm 1:1-3; 20:4; 37:4-6 & 23-24; 138:8

Romans 8:28-29; 12: 2

Timothy 2:20

1 Peter 1:3

CONFESSIONS FOR HEALING

Are you sick in your body? Feeling unwell? Been battling a disease for a while? Confess the Words below and receive your healing in Jesus name. When we make decrees for illness to leave our bodies, in the name of Jesus, sickness or ill-health must go.

In Habakkuk 2:4, we are told ...*but the just shall live by his faith*. Faith in believing that what you have said shall be so or shall come to pass. In 2 Corinthians 5:7 we are told that '*we walk by faith, not by sight;*' meaning as children of God, our starting point is to have faith, a place of trust and a place of believing God's Word.

Declaration:

My healing is a finished work that Jesus paid for on the Cross of Calvary. Father I thank you because you are the Alpha and Omega, the beginning and the end of all things. Forgive me Lord, for I have sinned against you and done that which is evil in your sight. I ask that you have mercy upon me. The Lord forgives all my iniquities and heals all my diseases and you redeem my life from the pit and crown me with love and compassion.

He sent His Word and healed me, and delivered me from destruction. I confess that by your stripes, I am healed. I thank you Lord Jesus that you are my passover and also you became a sacrifice for me and as such I decree that ill health (name the sickness) is not my portion in Jesus name.

Heal me O Lord and I shall be healed, save me O Lord and I shall be saved; you Lord sustain me upon my sickbed and in my illness you restore my health. Your Word tells me that you will take away from me all sickness and the grievous infirmities of Egypt. I will serve you Lord and you will bless my bread and water and take sickness away from me. I shall not die but live to declare the works of the Lord.

Father I am weary and burdened, please give me rest. Lord Jesus you bore my sins, on your body on the cross, so that I might die to sins and live for righteousness; by your wounds I am healed.

I pray all may go well with me, that I may be in good health, even as my soul prospers. As I fear your name, let the sun of righteousness arise with healing in its wings.

Have mercy on me, Lord, for I am faint; heal me, Lord, for my bones are in agony. Lord heal me with your hand. Father strengthen me and help me; uphold me with your righteous right hand.

Lord be gracious to me, I long for you. Be my strength every morning, my salvation in time of distress. Father, I hope in you, renew my strength. If I confess my sins, you Lord are faithful and just and you will forgive me from my sins and purify me from all unrighteousness.

Jesus thank you for taking away my infirmities and for bearing my disease, my High Priest, thank you for being touched by my infirmity.

Thank you that I called to you Lord and you healed me. Thank you Lord for restoring my health and allowing me to live, in Jesus name, amen. I shall not die, but live, and declare the works of the Lord. Father, as I have made the above Godly declaration, let it be so in Jesus name, amen.

If I diligently listen to the voice of the Lord my God and do what is right in His sight, give ear to His commandments and keep all His statutes, then God will not put any of the diseases on me which He brought on the Egyptians.

By the power in the Blood of Jesus, I command every organ in my body to be made whole. Lord as I have spoken your Word, hasten to perform your words in my life because the Word of God is living and powerful.

Prayer:

Father restore my health and heal my wounds in the name of Jesus.

Father Lord heal me as you healed blind Bartimeus.

Lord Jesus, the woman with the issue of blood touched the hem of your garment and received her healing immediately, Father do so for me, heal me now in Jesus name.

Reference:

Deuteronomy 7:15

Exodus 23:25

Hebrews 4:15

Jeremiah 17:14; 30:17

Isaiah 33:2; 41:10; 53:5; 38:16

Job 5:18

Matthew 8:17; 11:28

Psalms 6: 2; 30:2; 41:3; 51:4; 103:3; 107:20; 118:7

Revelation 22:13

1 Corinthians 5:7

3 John 1:2

2nd Peter 2:24

DECLARATIONS FOR PROTECTION – PSALM 91

This Psalm is a psalm of safety and when you feel safe, you will feel protected too. It was a psalm written by Moses, written to guarantee protection for the children of God in all ages; of God's fate in our earthly journey of life. God takes care of those who believe in Him, abide in Him and love Him. The most secure place in the world is under the shadow of the Almighty.

Tola's personalized version:

As I dwell in the secret place of the Most High

I shall abide under the shadow of the Almighty.

2 I will say of the Lord, "You are my refuge and my fortress; My God, in You I will trust."

3 Surely He shall deliver me from the snare of the fowler And from the perilous pestilence.

4 He shall cover me with His feathers,

And under His wings I will take refuge;

His truth shall be my shield and buckler.

5 I will not be afraid of the terror by night,

Nor of the arrow that flies by day,

6 Nor of the pestilence that walks in darkness,

Nor of the destruction that lays waste at noonday.

⁷ A thousand may fall at my side,

And ten thousand at my right hand;

But it shall not come near me.

⁸ Only with my eyes will I look,

And see the reward of the wicked.

⁹ Because I have made the Lord, who is my refuge,

Even the Most High, my dwelling place,

¹⁰ No evil shall befall me,

Nor shall any plague come near my dwelling;

¹¹ For He shall give His angels charge over me,

To keep me in all my ways.

¹² In their hands they shall bear me up,

Lest I dash my foot against a stone.

¹³ I will tread upon the lion and the cobra,

The young lion and the serpent I will trample underfoot.

¹⁴ "Because he/she has set his/her love upon Me, therefore I will deliver him/her; I will set him/her on high, because he/she has known My name.

¹⁵ He/She shall call upon Me, and I will answer him/her; I will be with him/her in trouble;

I will deliver him/her and honor him/her.

¹⁶ With long life I will satisfy him/her,

·And show him/her My salvation."

DEUTERONOMY 28:3-13 BLESSINGS

People might say that some of these Scriptures are solely for the children of Israel. I believed so too, until I read Ephesians 2:8 *For it is by grace (God's unmerited favor) that you are saved (delivered from judgment and made partakers of Christ's salvation) through faith (belief in God). And this (salvation) is not of yourselves (you didn't make it happen), but it is the gift of God.* This verse settled the matter for me as I believe that it is by grace through faith that we are partakers of Abraham's blessings.

Galatians 3: 26 *For you are all the children of God by faith in Christ Jesus.*

Contemporary English Version

Tola's personalised version:

³ The Lord will make my businesses and my farms (work) to be successful.

⁴ I will have many children. I will harvest large crops, and my herds of cattle and flocks of sheep and goats will produce many young.

⁵ I will have plenty of bread to eat.

6 The Lord will make me successful in my daily work.

7 The Lord will help me defeat my enemies and make them scatter in all directions.

8 The Lord my God is giving me the land, and He will make sure I am successful in everything I do. My harvests will be so large that my storehouses (bank accounts) will be full.

9 If I follow and obey the Lord, he will make me His own special people, just as He promised.

10 Then everyone on earth will know that I belong to the Lord, and they will be afraid of me.

11 The Lord will give me a lot of children and make sure that my animals give birth to many young. The Lord promised my ancestors that this land would be mine, and he will make it produce large crops (he will make it successful) for me.

¹² The Lord will open the storehouses of the skies where he keeps the rain, and he will send rain on my land (he will send shower of blessing on my work) at just the right times. He will make me successful in everything I do. I will have plenty of money to lend to other nations, but I won't need to borrow any myself.

¹³ I obey the laws and teachings that the Lord is giving me today, and the Lord my God will make me a leader among the nations, and not a follower. I will be wealthy and powerful, not poor and weak.

¹⁴ But I must not reject any of his laws and teachings or worship other gods.

PRIESTLY CONFESSIONS

Numbers 6:24-26

The Lord bless me and keep me;

The Lord make his face shine on me and be gracious to me;

The Lord turn his face toward me and give me peace.

PROSPERITY CONFESSIONS

We need to understand that when we make these prosperity confessions, we are declaring the word of God that tells us in 2 Corinthians 8: *⁹ For you know the grace of our Lord Jesus Christ, that though He was rich, yet for your sakes He became poor, that you through His poverty might become rich.* When we have this verse at the forefront of our minds, we can then focus on the authority given to us as we make these declarations in Jesus name.

In Matthew chapter 8:5-13, a centurion came to Jesus, telling him to pray for his servant. Jesus then said to the centurion that he would come with the centurion. But the man said no, he told Jesus in verse 8 *The centurion answered and said, "Lord, I am not worthy that You should come under my roof. <u>But only speak a word, and my servant will be healed.</u>* The centurion understood the importance of the spoken word. The centurion had great faith.

Proverb 13:22 states - *But the wealth of the sinner is stored up for the righteous.* Let us start by pleading the Blood of Jesus and asking Jesus to forgive us regarding how we have mismanaged money in the past.

Declarations:

The blessings of the Lord makes rich and adds no sorrow. Blessed be the Lord who daily loads me with benefits. And my God will supply every need of mine, according to his riches in glory in Christ Jesus. I submit to God and I am at peace with Him and in this way, prosperity will come to me. I will remember the Lord my God for it is He who gives me the power to get wealth.

Lord help me to keep your covenant and do them, so that I may prosper in all that I do. This Bible shall not depart from my mouth, but I will meditate in it day and night, that I may observe to do according to all that is written in it. For then I will make my way prosperous, and then I will have good success. I have given and it shall be given back to me in good measure, pressed down, shaken together and running over in Jesus name.

Lord I want to obey and serve you so that I can spend my days in prosperity and my years in pleasure. You Lord have come that I may have life and have it abundantly. Save now, Lord I pray, send now prosperity.

Holy Spirit help me seek God for as long as I seek God, the Lord will prosper me. Lord give me the treasures of darkness and hidden riches of secret places. And you Lord shall bless me because I am righteous and will surround me with favour like a shield.

Father my God, teach me to profit and lead me in the way I should go. I ... (your name) will flourish like the palm tree and grow like the cedar in Lebanon. I have planted in the house of God and will flourish in the courts of God; I will bring forth fruit in old age and I shall be fat and flourishing. You Lord will make me lay down in green pastures and my cup will overflow in Jesus name. Lord you became poor so that I might be rich, let the wealth of the sinner come to me in Jesus name.

Wealth and riches shall be in my house and my righteousness endures forever. The Word of the Lord stands forever. He who promised is faithful. The word of God is quick and powerful. I ... (your name) will prosper, if I am careful to observe the decrees and laws of God. My God shall answer my prayers because it is written that before I call, God will answer and while I am still speaking, He will hear me in Jesus name.

The Lord is my Shepherd and therefore I shall not lack in Jesus name. God gift me with riches and wealth, and the power to eat of it, to receive my heritage and rejoice in my labour in Jesus name.

By the grace of God, my way will prosper. I will thrive like a green leaf. Though my beginning was small, my latter end shall increase abundantly.

I (your name) will not lack any good thing. The Word of God stands forever. And I believe because He who promised is faithful.

Prayer:

Father Lord I am believing you for my financial breakthrough in Jesus name.

Father Lord bless me so I can be a blessing to others.

Father Lord, I can stand to be blessed financially in Jesus name.

References:

Deuteronomy 8:18a; 29:9

Ecclesiastes 5:19

Hebrews 10:23; 4:12a

Isaiah 40:8; 45:3; 48: 15& 17; 65:24

Job 8:7; 22:21; 36:11

John 10:10

Joshua 1:8

Luke 6:38

Philippians 4:19

Proverbs 10:22; 11:28; 13:22;

Psalms 5:12; 23: 1-2; 34:10; 68:19; 92:12-14, 112:3; 118:25

1 Chronicles 22:13

2 Chronicles 26:5

WARFARE DECLARATIONS

As a Christian, know that you are in a battle. Jesus when on earth had battles to fight. There is no way as a Christian that you will not have powers of darkness contending against one area of your life. There are so many Scriptures in the Bible that talk about fighting or about the enemy. God uses the negative experiences that we go through in life, in order to strengthen us as we become an enhanced tool in His Hands.

We are told to be sober and alert because our enemy the devil prowls around like a roaring lion looking for someone to devour. We are told to resist him, standing firm in the faith – 1 Peter 5:8-9

Declarations:

Thank you Lord that you have given me power to tread on serpents and scorpions, and over all the power of the enemy, and nothing shall by any means hurt me. Thank you Lord because for this reason the Son of God appeared, to destroy the devil's work.

No weapon fashioned against me shall prosper and every tongue that rises against me in judgement, I condemn. I submit myself to God, I resist the devil and he will flee from me. For though I walk in the flesh, I do not war according to the flesh. For the weapons of my warfare *are* not carnal but mighty in God for pulling down strongholds, casting down arguments and every high thing that exalts itself against the knowledge of God, bringing every thought into captivity to the obedience of Christ.

I am more than a conqueror through Him who loves me but thanks be to God, who gives me the victory through my Lord Jesus Christ. This battle I am going through (name it) is not by might nor by power, but by the Spirit of God, says the Lord of hosts.

But the Lord is faithful, and he will strengthen me and protect me from the evil one. And I have conquered him by the blood of the Lamb and by the word of my testimony, for I love not my life even unto death.

I thank you Lord, because you told me whatever I bind on earth will be bound in heaven, and whatever I loose on earth will be loosed in heaven.

I therefore bind (name it). The Lord will cause my enemies who rise against me to be defeated before me. They shall come out against me one way and flee before me seven ways.

Do not fear them (add your name), for the Lord my God is the one fighting for me. What then shall I say of these things? If God is for me, who is against me? Through you, I will push back my adversaries, through your name I will trample down those who rise up against me. For you have girded me with strength for battle; you have subdued under me those who rose up against me.

For I do not wrestle against flesh and blood, but against principalities, against powers, against the rulers of the darkness of this age, against spiritual hosts of wickedness in the heavenly places. For you have been a shelter for me, a strong tower from the enemy.

And from the days of John the Baptist until now the Kingdom of Heaven suffers violence and the violent take it by force; I therefore wage a good warfare in Jesus name.

Prayer:

As I go into spiritual battle, I put on the full armour of God (Ephesians 6:10-18)

By the power in the Blood of Jesus, I will overcome this battle (name it)

Let God arise and all my enemies be scattered in Jesus name.

Reference:

Deuteronomy 3:22; 28:7

Ephesians 6:12

Isaiah 54:17

James 4:7

John 10:10

Luke 10:19

Matthew 18:18

Psalms 18:39; 44:5; 61:3; 118:17

Revelation.12:11

Romans 8:37; 8:31

1 Corinthians 15:57

2 Corinthians 10:4; 10:3-5

1 John 3:8

2 Thessalonians 3:3

1 Timothy 1:18

Zechariah 4:6

PRAYER POINTS

Jesus said that whatsoever I shall ask in prayer, believing, I shall receive in Jesus name.

As you remembered Abraham for good, Lord remember me for good too in Jesus name.

I soak every organ in my body in the blood of Jesus and command them to work according to the precepts of God and not man in Jesus name.

I command full restoration of my health in Jesus name.

I am redeemed and an overcomer in Christ, I am not forsaken, I will not lack divine helpers in Jesus name.

I pray that the Lord will make a way for me where there seems to be no way in Jesus name.

Lord you were with Joseph and showed him mercy, I ask for such mercy in my life today and always in Jesus name.

I pray that the windows of Heaven will be opened onto me in Jesus name.

My enemies shall perish after the order of the Egyptian army at the Red sea in Jesus name.

Every Haman spirit contending with my life shall die in my place in Jesus name.

I decree that I will excel in life and do exploits in Jesus name.

My God is my source and He supplies all my needs in Jesus name.

I will no longer limit myself and failure is no longer my portion in Jesus name.

Lord, let mercy speak for me in the area of...(name the situation) in Jesus name.

Lord let protocol be broken for my sake in the name of Jesus.

Let grace propel me to where I do not think I can get to in Jesus name.

CONCLUSION

Throughout this book, I have used words such as decree, declaration, command, confession, etc. When you realise that what you are saying is based on Biblical truths, then your words will make your circumstance/s to change and improve. In order for the Kingdom of God to turn into your reality, don't forget in Jeremiah 29:11, God says, *For I know the thoughts that I think toward you, says the Lord, thoughts of peace and not of evil, to give you a future and a hope.*

We are making these confessions by faith in the name of our Lord Jesus Christ. We are told in Hebrews 11:30 *that by faith the walls of Jericho fell down, after they were compassed about seven days singing.* How can one defeat an enemy by singing? In the eyes of an unbeliever, this cannot be possible, but God. By faith, the children of Israel opened their mouths and were singing round that wall for seven days, till it fell down. You can read the story in Joshua chapter 6.

All you have been doing as you read this book, is help yourself in the area of making proclamations of purpose and declarations of truth.

The more you get into the habit of confessing God's Words, the more you are executing a spiritual decision in your favour with the authority of God. When we belong to Christ, the enemy never has the final word over our lives, Christ does because we are secure in God's hands.

What you are also doing is you are effecting the requirement and intention of God. Speaking God's Word gives us the guarantee, that when we quote Scripture, we are fulfilling the very will and purpose of God in our lives and situations.

The splendor in the Words of life that you speak is that they will destroy the plan of the enemy planned or perpetuated against you because God has put all things under our control from the book of Genesis.

In Job 22:28, It is written that *"You will also declare a thing, And it will be established for you; So light will shine on your ways."* The words that we speak have influence. The words that we declare have a purpose. Let us become more aware of what come out of our mouths.

God bless you richly and keep you in Jesus name.

ABOUT THE AUTHOR

Tola Dehinde has been a student in the area of Bible study for decades. Her love for God made her to start blogging on: www.pastors1stlady.co.uk

She has been pouring out spiritual nuggets at the onset on a weekly basis and later on a monthly basis for a long time.

Recently, she felt the leading of the Lord and also through close friends, telling her to turn her blog articles into books; she commenced the work of faith.

As Tola started, the Holy Spirit instructed her to look for all the articles that she had written over the years on prayer. She was able to find enough material to publish her first book: PRAYER PERSONIFIED.

Tola's hope is that this book will be a blessing to you as it has been to her, writing and reading it. She prays this book will help you to read and explore the Bible more, as she did, spending precious times in God's presence writing this book.

God bless and keep you well.

Other books by Tola Dehinde:

PRAYER PERSONIFIED – available on Amazon

Contact details: t.dehinde@yahoo.com

Printed in Great Britain
by Amazon

18549033R00036